It's full of friendly people.

The mail carrier delivers mail.

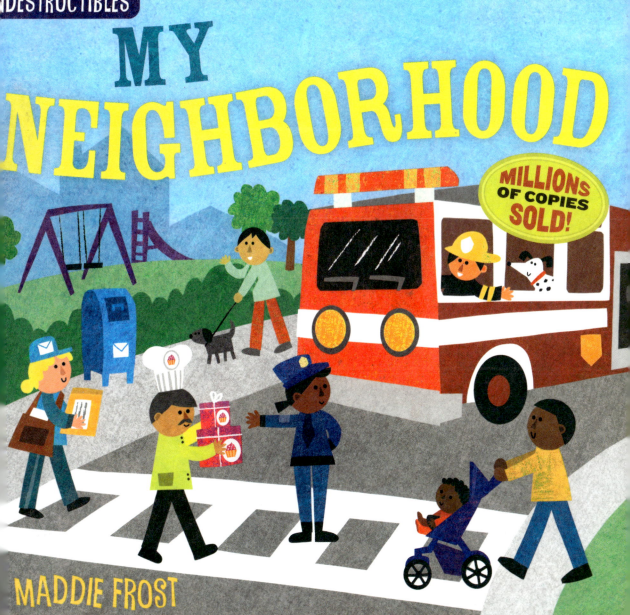

THE ORIGINAL INDESTRUCTIBLES®

Chew Proof • Rip Proof • Nontoxic • 100% Washable

MY NEIGHBORHOOD

MILLIONS OF COPIES SOLD!

MADDIE FROST

Welcome to my neighborhood!

The garbage collectors keep things clean.

The firefighters help those in trouble.

The police officer
keeps us safe.

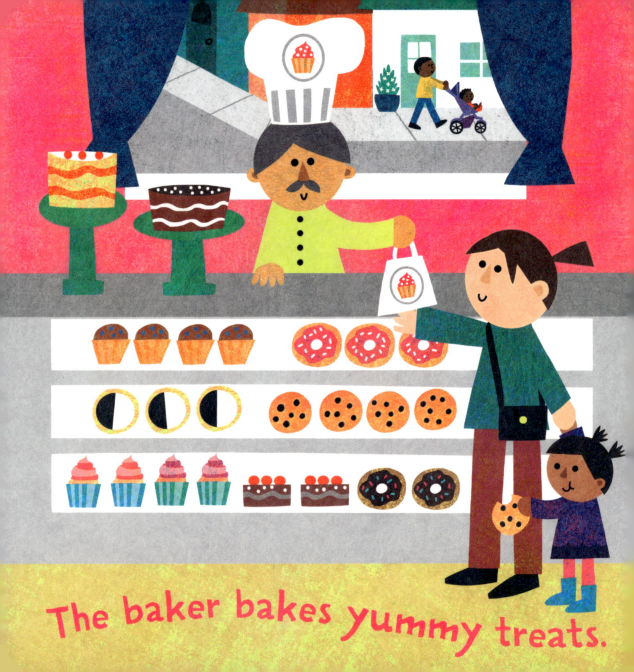

The baker bakes yummy treats.

The teacher shows us new things.

We all

help each other!

Books babies can really sink their gums into!

Here comes our mail. Thank you, mail carrier!
See how clean our street is. Thank you, garbage collector!
Say hello to everyone in the neighborhood.
We all help one another out!

Tour around town in a book that's INDESTRUCTIBLE.

DEAR PARENTS: INDESTRUCTIBLES are built for the way babies "read": with their hands and mouths. INDESTRUCTIBLES won't rip or tear and are 100% washable. They're made for baby to hold, grab, chew, pull, and bend.

CHEW ALL THESE AND MORE!

$5.99 US / $7.99 Can.
ISBN 978-1-5235-0469-5

9 781523 504695   50599

Copyright © 2018 by Indestructibles, LLC. Used under license. Illustrations copyright © 2018 by Workman Publishing. All rights reserved. Library of Congress Cataloging-in-Publication Data is available. Workman Kids is an imprint of Workman Publishing, a division of Hachette Book Group, Inc. The Workman name and logo are registered trademarks of Hachette Book Group, Inc.

Distributed in the United Kingdom by Hachette Book Group, UK, Carmelite House, 50 Victoria Embankment, London EC4Y 0DZ. Distributed in Europe by Hachette Livre, 58 rue Jean Bleuzen, 92 178 Vanves Cedex, France. Contact special.markets@hbgusa.com regarding special discounts for bulk purchases.

All INDESTRUCTIBLES books have been safety-tested and meet or exceed ASTM-F963 and CPSIA guidelines. INDESTRUCTIBLES is a registered trademark of Indestructibles, LLC. Cover © 2024 Hachette Book Group, Inc. First Edition August 2018 | 10 9 8 7 Printed in China | IMFP

WORKMAN PUBLISHING • Hachette Book Group, Inc., 1290 Avenue of the Americas, New York, NY 10104 • indestructiblesinc.com